Care Bears
Christmas Wishes

By Ellie O'Ryan
Illustrated by Saxton Moore

Designed by Michael Massen
No part of this publication may be reproduced in whole or in part, or stored in a retrieval system,
or transmitted in any form or by any means, electronic, mechanical, photocopying, recording, or
otherwise, without written permission of the publisher. For information regarding permission, write to
Scholastic Inc., Attention: Permissions Department, 557 Broadway, New York, NY 10012.
ISBN 0-439-78541-3
12 11 10 9 8 7 6 5 4 3 2   5 6 7 8 9/0
Printed in the U.S.A.
First printing, November 2005

SCHOLASTIC INC.
New York   Toronto   London   Auckland   Sydney
Mexico City   New Delhi   Hong Kong   Buenos Aires

It was Christmastime in Care-a-lot!
Christmas was Wish Bear's favorite time of year.

Wish Bear wrote her friends' names on a list.
"This is going to be the best Christmas ever,"
she said to herself. "I can't wait to make all my
friends' Christmas wishes come true!"

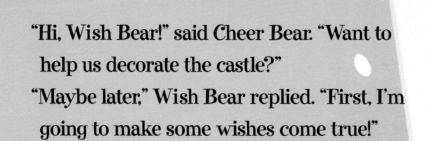

"Hi, Wish Bear!" said Cheer Bear. "Want to help us decorate the castle?"

"Maybe later," Wish Bear replied. "First, I'm going to make some wishes come true!"

Wish Bear hurried outside into the cold.

"Wish Bear, wait!" Cheer Bear called after her.
"You forgot your hat and scarf!"
But Wish Bear was already gone.

First on the list was Bedtime Bear. "I know just the thing—an alarm clock!" Wish Bear exclaimed. "Now Bedtime Bear can take a long nap without worrying that he'll oversleep."

"This sled will help Champ Care Bear have fun in the snow," Wish Bear said. "And I can carry all the other presents on it until I get home!"

Funshine Bear was next on the list. "A funny joke book will help Funshine Bear do his favorite thing—make people laugh!" said Wish Bear.

"A bunch of rainbow flowers will make Cheer Bear even more cheery," Wish Bear said. "And Grumpy Bear won't feel so down when he looks at this picture of his best friends."

"Brrrr!" Wish Bear shivered as the snow fell faster. "It's f-f-frosty out. That gives me an idea—a milkshake cup for two is the perfect present for Share Bear. Then she can share with everyone!"

Then Wish Bear's nose started feeling tickly and her throat started feeling scratchy. *"Ah-ah-ah-choo!"* she sneezed. "I don't feel very well," Wish Bear said sadly. "And I'm too tired to finish gathering everyone's Christmas wishes."

Back at the castle, the Care Bears were happy to see
Wish Bear—but she wasn't feeling happy at all.
"What's the matter, Wish Bear?" asked
Tenderheart Bear.

"I didn't finish making everyone's Christmas wishes come true," Wish Bear said sadly. "And—*ah-ah-ah-choo!*—I think I caught a cold. Christmas is ruined!"

"No it isn't!" exclaimed Cheer Bear. "Christmas is about caring. And caring for a friend in need is something Care Bears do best!"

"Poor Wish Bear," said Love-a-lot Bear. "You need some tender loving care to get over that cold."

"But what about your Christmas wishes?" Wish Bear asked.

"Leave that to us!" Champ Care Bear announced.

The Care Bears went right to work.
"This cozy blanket will warm you right up!" Tenderheart Bear
said as he tucked Wish Bear into bed.

"Have some yummy soup," suggested Share Bear.
"I made it myself!"

Love-a-lot Bear brought Wish Bear a glass of juice.
"This will help your scratchy throat," she said.

And Funshine Bear told a funny story that
made Wish Bear smile.

Bedtime Bear fluffed Wish Bear's pillow. "Sweet dreams, Wish Bear," he whispered. "I hope you feel better in the morning!"

The Care Bears tiptoed out of Wish Bear's room just as
Grumpy Bear, Good Luck Bear, and Champ Care Bear
returned to the castle with the last of the Christmas presents.

When Wish Bear woke up the next morning, she *did* feel a lot better!

"Merry Christmas, everybody!" Wish Bear said. "Thank you for taking such good care of me. I'm sorry that I didn't make all of your Christmas wishes come true."

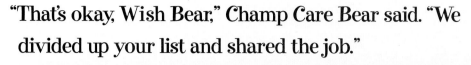

"That's okay, Wish Bear," Champ Care Bear said. "We divided up your list and shared the job."

"Besides, the most important Christmas wish was for you to feel better," Love-a-lot Bear added. "And now you do!"

It was a very merry Christmas in Care-a-lot—full of
sharing, caring, and Christmas wishes come true!